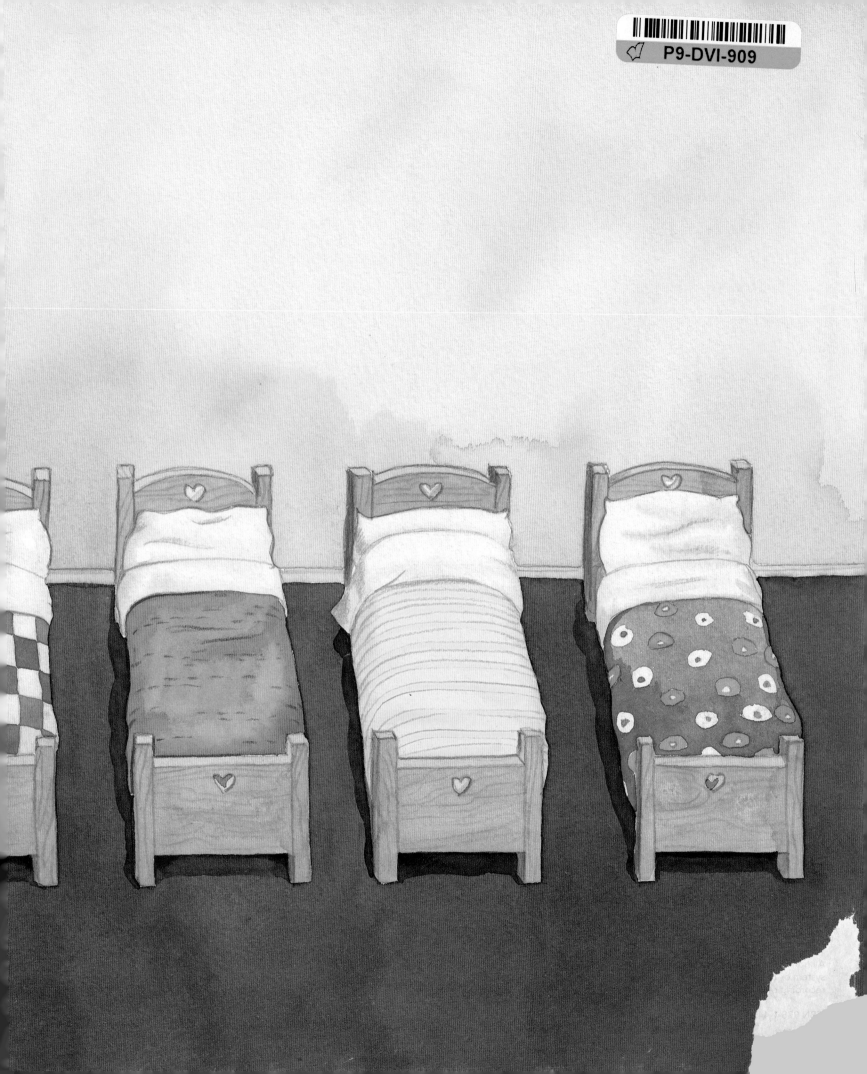

This edition published by Parragon in 2012
Parragon
Queen Street House
4 Queen Street
Bath BA1 1HE, UK
www.parragon.com

ISBN 978-1-4454-7699-5

Snow White
and the Seven Dwarfs

Retold by Ronne Randall

Illustrated by Jacqueline East

PaRragon

Bath • New York • Singapore • Hong Kong • Cologne • Delhi
Melbourne • Amsterdam • Johannesburg • Auckland • Shenzhen

One snowy winter's day, a queen sat sewing by her window.

She accidentally pricked her finger with the needle, and three drops of blood fell on the snow that had fallen on the black wooden window ledge. The Queen sighed and thought "I wish I had a child with lips as red as blood, skin as white as snow, and hair as black as ebony wood!"

Some time after that, the Queen gave birth to a little girl with deep red lips, snowy white skin, and glossy hair as black as ebony. She named her Snow White.

Sadly, the Queen died and the King married again. His new wife was beautiful, but cruel. She had a magic mirror, and every day she looked into it and asked,

"Mirror, mirror, on the wall, Who is the fairest one of all?"

And every day the mirror replied,

"You, O Queen, are the fairest of all."

One morning, however, the Queen's mirror said to her,

"You, O Queen,
are fair, it's true.
But Snow White
is much fairer
than you!"

Snow White had grown up into a beautiful young girl.
In a jealous rage, the Queen called her huntsman.

"I never want to see Snow White's face again,"
she told him. "Take her into the forest and kill her."

The huntsman was a good man and could not bear to hurt Snow White.

"Run away, child," he said. "Don't ever come back, or the Queen will kill you."

Snow White was very frightened, but she did as the huntsman said.

Toward nightfall, Snow White came to a little cottage deep in the woods. She knocked softly, but there was no answer, so she let herself in.

Inside, Snow White found a table and seven tiny chairs. Upstairs there were seven little beds.

She lay down on a bed and soon fell fast asleep.

A while later, she woke with a start. Seven little men were standing around her bed.

"Who are you?" she asked.

"We are the seven dwarfs who live here," said one of the little men. "Who are YOU?"

"I am Snow White," she replied, and she told them her sad story.

The dwarfs felt sorry for Snow White and they wanted to help.

"If you will cook and clean for us," said the eldest dwarf, "you can stay here and we will keep you safe."

Snow White gratefully agreed. When they left for work the next morning, the dwarfs made Snow White promise not to go out, or open the door, or speak to anyone.

Meanwhile, the Queen was back at her
magic mirror. But she was shocked by what
it told her,

"You are the fairest here, it's true,
But there is someone fairer than you.
Deep in the forest, in a cozy den,
Snow White lives with
seven little men."

"What?" shrieked the Queen. "Snow White
is ALIVE?"

In a wild frenzy, the Queen, who was really
a wicked witch, brewed a deadly potion and
poisoned a rosy, red apple.

Disguising herself as an old pedlar woman,
she set out for the cottage where the seven
dwarfs lived.

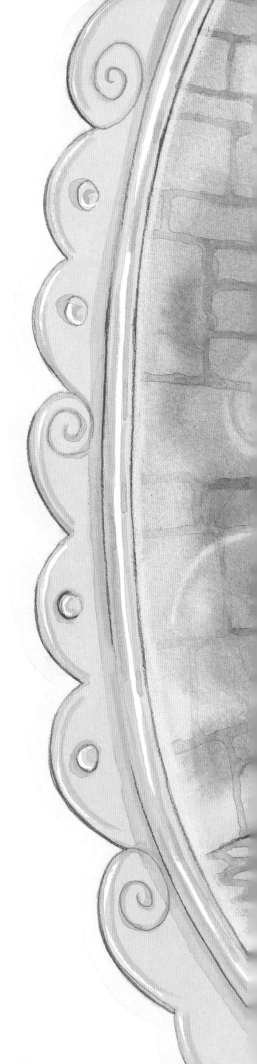

When the wicked Queen reached the little cottage, she knocked on the door.

"Apples for sale," she croaked. "Try my lovely red apples!" And she handed the poisoned apple to Snow White.

Snow White couldn't resist. She took a big bite …

… and

fell

down,

to the floor.

The delighted Queen hurried
home to talk to her magic mirror.

"You, O Queen,
are the
fairest of all!"

The dwarfs wept bitterly when they came home to find Snow White lying totally still on the cottage floor.

They carefully laid her in a glass case and watched over her, day and night.

One day a prince came riding through the forest. When he saw the beautiful girl in the glass case, he fell in love with her.

"Please let me take her back to my castle," he begged the dwarfs. They agreed.

As the dwarfs lifted the glass case, the prince kissed Snow White. Suddenly Snow White gasped out loud!

"Please don't be frightened," said the prince. "You are with someone who loves you more than life itself. Will you marry me?"

Snow White looked into the prince's kind, gentle eyes and knew that she loved him, too. "Yes," she said. "I will."

Snow White and the prince were married.
They lived happily ever after, together with
the dwarfs, in the prince's castle.

The End

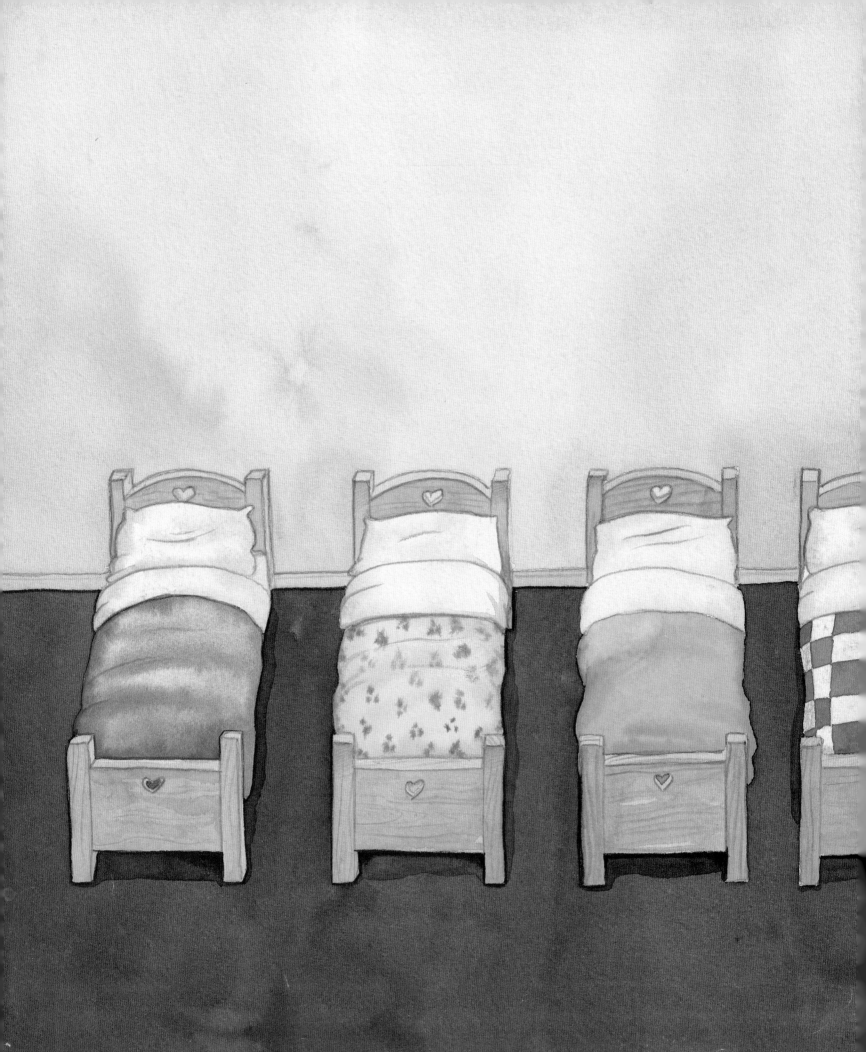